D0835630

Amy's Slippers

First published 2007
Evans Brothers Limited
2A Portman Mansions
Chiltern Street
London W1U 6NR

British Library Cataloguing in Publication Data

Chapman, Mary
  Amy's slippers. - (Spirals)
  1. Children's stories
  I. Title
  823.9'2[J]

ISBN-13: 9780237533533 (HB)
ISBN-13: 9780237533472 (PB)

Printed in China

Series Editor: Nick Turpin
Design: Robert Walster
Production: Jenny Mulvanny

Amy's Slippers

Mary Chapman
and Simona Dimitri

Evans

Mum groaned.

'Amy! There's mud all over the floor!'

'Sorry,' said Amy.

'That's three times this week,' said Mum. 'Take your shoes off. Don't move until I've cleared it up. Then PUT ON YOUR SLIPPERS!'

'Can't find them,' said Amy. 'They're always going missing. I wish I had some magic ones.'

'Don't be silly,' said Mum.

'They'd know when I wanted them,' said Amy dreamily, 'and they'd come and find me.'

'Nonsense!' said Mum.

Next day when Amy got home
from school there, on the doormat,
was a pair of new slippers – pink
and sparkly!

'Thanks, Mum.'

'I don't know where they've come
from,' said Mum, puzzled.

Amy put them on.

They fitted perfectly.

The next afternoon when school finished Amy's slippers were at the school gates.

'They've come to meet you,' laughed Rosie.

Amy went red.

She stuffed them into her bag.

When she got home she gave them A GOOD TELLING-OFF.

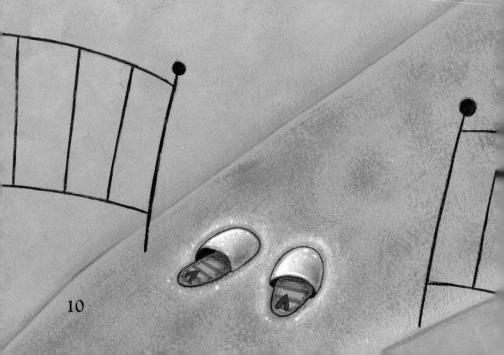

11

Next morning, when she arrived at school, they were on her desk.

'You know you don't bring slippers to school, Amy,' said Miss Green.

Everybody laughed.

When she went to bed Amy put the slippers in her wardrobe, and turned the key.

13

Squeak, squeak, scrabble, scrabble.

Amy woke with a jump.

She shot out of bed.

The wardrobe was rocking backwards and forwards.

The door burst open.

Out leapt her slippers.

They skipped towards her and slipped onto her feet.

They walked her to the door, down the stairs, out of the house, and into the street.

Her slippers weren't pink and sparkling anymore.

They were white.

They'd turned into trainers!

They were running, faster and faster!

Houses and hedges, bushes and trees flashed by.

She whizzed along so fast she soon left the streets behind.

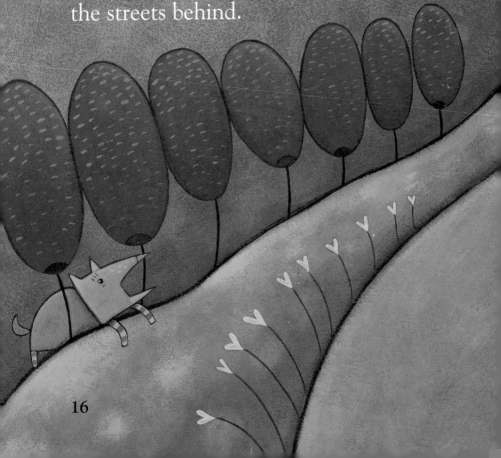

There was grass beneath her feet.
She was wearing football boots!
The ball hurtled towards her.
She stopped it neatly, turned and
sprinted with it down the pitch.
She aimed at the goal and kicked the
ball, straight into the back of the net!
YES!

She was in the country now,
in a big open space.
A frozen lake.
Her boots had turned into
elegant skates.
She skimmed across the ice.

Above her, dark sky, bright stars.
Around her, snowy mountains.
The icy lake rose and fell.
Then tilted and tipped, and plunged
her down the mountainside.

23

She was skiing, weaving in and out.
The wind rushed past.
The snow glittered.
She jumped.
She was leaping across a gaping
crevasse...

...and diving – into the sea.
She tasted salt water.
Flippers moved her legs up and down.
Stripy fish and silvery fish darted
amongst coral branches and gently
waving fronds, rainbow-coloured.
A dark shadow loomed.

Amy opened her eyes.

The wardrobe door was open.

Her slippers were by her bed.

She slid her feet into them, and ran
downstairs to tell Mum what had
happened.

'Don't be silly, Amy,' said Mum.
'You've been dreaming.'

Amy knew she hadn't.

She wriggled her toes in her
slippers.

They were still cold and damp.

Why not try reading a Spirals book?

Megan's Tick Tock Rocket by Andrew Fusek Peters,
Polly Peters, and Simona Dimitri
ISBN 978 0237 53342 7

Growl! by Vivian French and Tim Archbold
ISBN 978 0237 53345 8

John and the River Monster by Paul Harrison
and Ian Benfold Haywood
ISBN 978 0237 53344 1

Froggy Went a Hopping by Alan Durant and Sue Mason
ISBN 978 0237 53346 5

Glub! By Penny Little and Sue Mason
ISBN 978 0237 53461 5

Amy's Slippers by Mary Chapman and Simona Dimitri
ISBN 978 0237 53347 2

The Grumpy Queen by Valerie Wilding
and Simona Sanfilippo
ISBN 978 0237 53459 2

The Flamingo Who Forgot by Alan Durant
and Franco Rivolli
ISBN 978 0237 53343 4